Henrietta and the HAT

by Mabel Watts

illustrated by Jane Miller

PARENTS' MAGAZINE PRESS, INC.
52 Vanderbilt Ave., New York 17, N. Y.

Library of Congress Catalog Card Number: 62-12944. Printed in the U. S. A.

HENRIETTA AND THE HAT

One day long ago Farmer Flinders bought a new hat.

It was a sort of chocolate-colored hat, with a band of ribbon on it, and a small red feather sticking up on one side.

Henrietta the horse took a great fancy to Farmer Flinders' hat, right from the start.

"If only I had a hat like that," she said.

But Henrietta did not get the hat, in spite of all her wishes. Instead, she got a nice bag of oats every day.

Farmer Flinders wore that chocolate-colored hat for a long, long time.

He wore it to church. And to market. And when he went to visit folks on Sunday afternoons.

He wore it to taffy-pulls and
corn-popping parties.

He wore it to rodeos and roundups.

He wore it to the circus and the fair.

Farmer Flinders wore that hat
just about everywhere.

"Such a pretty hat," Henrietta always said when she saw it. "How I wish that it were mine!"

She said it every time she pulled Farmer Flinders along in the little buggy.

But Henrietta did not get the hat, in

spite of all her wishes. Instead, she got a nice knob of sugar every day.

As time went on the sun shone down on the farmer's hat quite a lot. The winds blew on it, the rains rained on it and the snows snowed on it.

Sometimes Jack Frost whitened up the small red feather a bit.

And by and by the chocolate-colored hat began to look a little shabby.

That was when Farmer Flinders gave the hat to Mrs. Flinders.

Mrs. Flinders wore the hat when she fed the chickens, when she picked the roses and when she weeded the vegetable garden.

Henrietta often saw the hat perched on Mrs. Flinders' head.

Certainly the feather had faded some. The ribbon was frayed a little. And the battered brim was beginning to curl up at the edges.

But to Henrietta the chocolate-colored hat was still the most beautiful hat in the whole wide world.

"Such a wonderful hat," she sighed.

But Henrietta did not get the hat, in spite of all her wishes. Instead, she got a carrot every day.

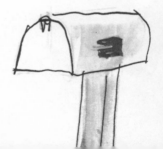

Then one day Mrs. Flinders took a peek at herself in the mirror, wearing the hat.

"Dear, dear!" she said. "This hat is not the least bit becoming to me!"

And Mrs. Flinders took off the hat.

That was when Freddy Flinders began using the hat to gather the eggs.

Freddy gathered lots and lots of eggs in the old hat. Bantam eggs, medium-sized eggs and large eggs. White eggs, speckled eggs and brown eggs.

Often as not, Henrietta saw Freddy as he carried the hat, full of eggs, from the barn to the kitchen door.

"How truly lovely that hat would look on me!" sighed the horse.

But Henrietta did not get the hat, in spite of all her wishes. Instead, she got a pat on the back every day.

Then one day...splat! An egg fell through
the side of the old hat.

"There's a hole in this hat," Freddy said.
"I can't use it any more for gathering eggs!"

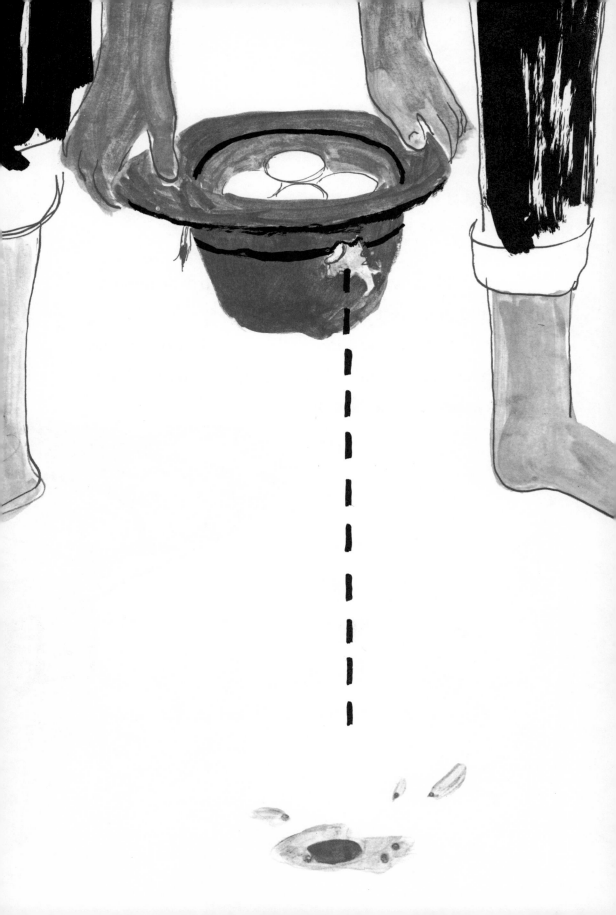

That was when a mother bird decided to build her nest in the hat.

How busy that mother bird was as she flitted here and there carrying leaves and grasses to line the hat.

Then the mother bird laid four pale blue eggs in it.

By this time the hat had grown flattish and floppy. But it still looked pretty to Henrietta, even when the mother bird nested inside it.

"If only I had a hat like that," she said, "I'd be the best-looking horse in town!"

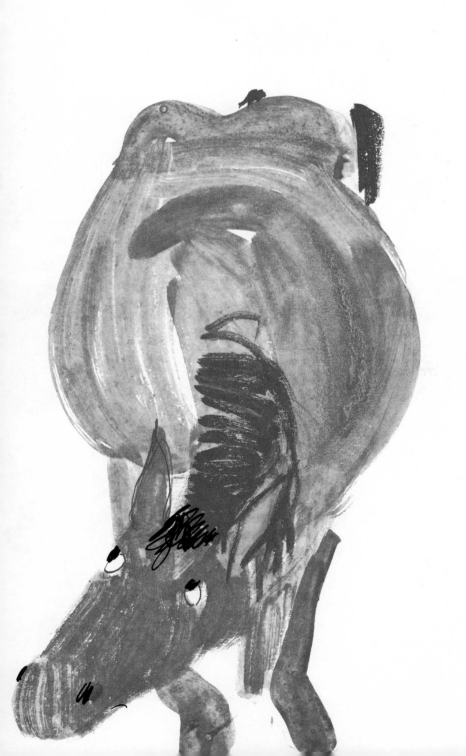

But Henrietta did not get the hat, in spite of all her wishes. Instead, she got a bed of sweet-smelling hay to sleep on.

The chocolate-colored hat made a snug home for the mother bird and her four little baby birds.

Every morning the mother bird went out to look for worms and grubs to feed her family. And oh, how those baby birds could eat!

They ate and they ate . . . and they grew.

They grew right out of the chocolate-colored hat!

PEEP

Then one day the whole bird family flew south for the winter. And there was the old hat without an owner once more.

The hat was drab and rusty, and to Freddy it looked for all the world like an old dishpan.

But Henrietta thought it looked perkier than ever.

"Look," said Farmer Flinders. "The hat has two holes in it now, instead of one."

Freddy looked at the two holes. Then he looked at Henrietta. He looked especially at her long ears.

That was when Freddy put the hat on Henrietta's head.

Henrietta had waited a long time for that chocolate-colored hat, and now she had it AT LAST!

The hat was too shabby for Farmer Flinders
to wear now.

It was not stylish enough for Mrs. Flinders.

It was no good for gathering eggs.

The mother bird didn't want it any more.

But the chocolate-colored hat fitted Henrietta
like a charm.

The old horse tossed her head and laughed her
high-up happy laugh.

She knew she was the best-looking horse in town!

THE END